A Duck, Duck, Porcupine! Book

That's My Book!

And Other Stories

Salina Yoon

BLOOMSBURY

NEW YORK LONDON OXFORD NEW DELHI SYDNEY

For Penguin

First published in the United States of America in September 2017
by Bloomsbury Children's Books
www.bloomsbury.com

Bloomsbury is a registered trademark of Bloomsbury Publishing Plc

For information about permission to reproduce selections from this book, write to
Permissions, Bloomsbury Children's Books, 1385 Broadway, New York, New York 10018
Bloomsbury books may be purchased for business or promotional use. For information on bulk purchases please
contact Macmillan Corporate and Premium Sales Department at specialmarkets@macmillan.com

Library of Congress Cataloging-in-Publication Data
available upon request
ISBN 978-1-61963-891-4 (hardcover) • ISBN 978-1-61963-892-1 (e-book) • ISBN 978-1-61963-893-8 (e-PDF)

Art created digitally using Adobe Photoshop
Typeset in Cronos Pro
Book design by Salina Yoon and Jeanette Levy
Printed in China by Leo Paper Products, Heshan, Guangdong
3 5 7 9 10 8 6 4 2

All papers used by Bloomsbury Publishing, Inc., are natural, recyclable products
made from wood grown in well-managed forests. The manufacturing processes
conform to the environmental regulations of the country of origin.

Three Short Stories

One
That's My Book!

Two
Let's Have a Talent Show!

Three
Dress-Like-a-Pirate Day

One

That's My Book!

Two

Let's Have a Talent Show!

Three

Dress-Like-a-Pirate Day